Ready or Not, Woolbur Goes to School!!

by LESLIE HELAKOSKI
pictures by LEE HARPER

HARPER
An Imprint of HarperCollinsPublishers

To Judy Bryan, Carrie Pearson, Kelly Bennett,
and Marty Graham,
aren't they great?
—Leslie

To Dan, the Woolbur of our family
—Lee

AUG 1 7 2018

Ready or Not, Woolbur Goes to School!
Text copyright © 2018 by Leslie Helakoski
Illustrations copyright © 2018 by Lee Harper
All rights reserved. Manufactured in China.
No part of this book may be used or reproduced in any manner whatsoever without written permission except in the case of
brief quotations embodied in critical articles and reviews. For information address HarperCollins Children's Books,
a division of HarperCollins Publishers, 195 Broadway, New York, NY 10007.
www.harpercollinschildrens.com

ISBN 978-0-06-136657-4

The artist used watercolor and pencil on 140 lb cold press watercolor paper to create the illustrations for this book.
18 19 20 21 22   SCP   10 9 8 7 6 5 4 3 2 1
❖
First Edition

"It's the first day of school!" said Woolbur.

"Let's go!"

"I'm not sure Woolbur's ready for school," said Maa.

"I'm not sure school's ready for Woolbur!" said Paa.

"I'm ready," said Woolbur. "I can dress myself and fix my wool."

"No one else will look like you do," said Maa.

"Your wool is a little unusual," said Paa.

"I know," said Woolbur.

"Isn't it great?"

Maa and Paa took deep breaths and walked Woolbur to school.

"I can write my own name," said Woolbur.

"You used a lot of shapes and swirls!" said Maa.
"No one can tell what it says!" said Paa.

"I know," said Woolbur.

"Isn't it great?"

Maa and Paa took deep breaths
and headed for the door.

"Don't worry,"
said the teacher.
"He's ready for school."

"I can paint pictures," said Woolbur.

"But we can't tell if this is upside down or right side up," said Dog. "And you've colored outside the lines!"

"I know," said Woolbur. "Isn't it great?"

"I can wait my turn," said Woolbur.
"But there are so many of us," said Llama.
"And we have to share with everybody!"

"I know," said Woolbur.

"Isn't it great?"

"I can eat lunch in the cafeteria," said Woolbur.

"It smells weird in here," said Goat.

"And the grass tastes different than it does at home."

"I know," said Woolbur.

"Isn't it great?"

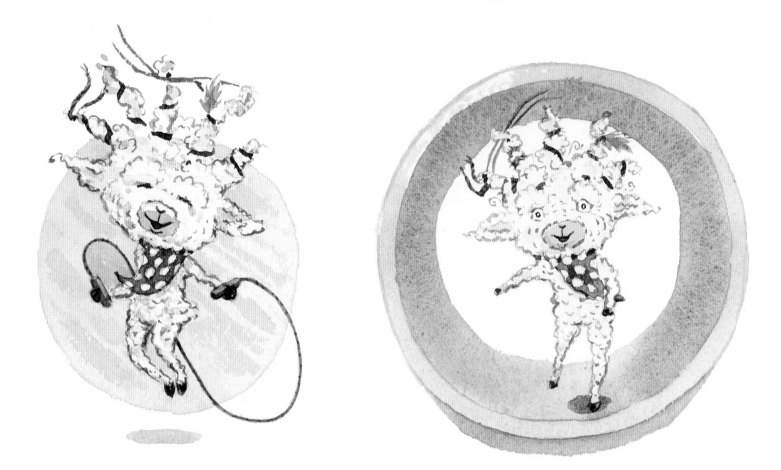

"I can run and jump on the playground," said Woolbur.

"It sure is noisy out here," said Donkey.

"And I've never played these games before."

"I know," said Woolbur. **"Isn't it great?"**

"I can ride the bus home," said Woolbur.

"But it's filled with kids I don't know," said Pig.

"And I've never heard some of these words before."

"I know," said Woolbur.

"Isn't it great?"

"I'm back!" said Woolbur hopping off the bus.
"I can't wait for tomorrow!"

"Maybe you are ready," said Maa.

"I'm ready for school," said Woolbur. "Are you ready?"

"Ready for what?" asked Maa.

"A home-again kiss!" said Woolbur.

"Woolbur's growing up," said Paa.

"Yes he is," said Maa.

"Isn't it great?"